SUPER SOLVE IT™

Puzzles, Mazes, Word Games, and More!

Text by Daniel Wallace

studio fun

A READER'S DIGEST COMPANY

White Plains, New York • Montréal, Québec • Bath, United Kingdom

LOTHAL MAZES

Zeb is trying to rescue Ezra from a prison cell deep inside an Imperial Star Destroyer. Imperial stormtroopers are everywhere, and he has to be careful! Help Zeb by finding the path that takes him from START to END. You can only exit through one of the metal triangles in each hexagon. The legend on the left shows you which direction each triangle will send you next. You must go through the space with the rebel symbol before you reach the END.

START

END

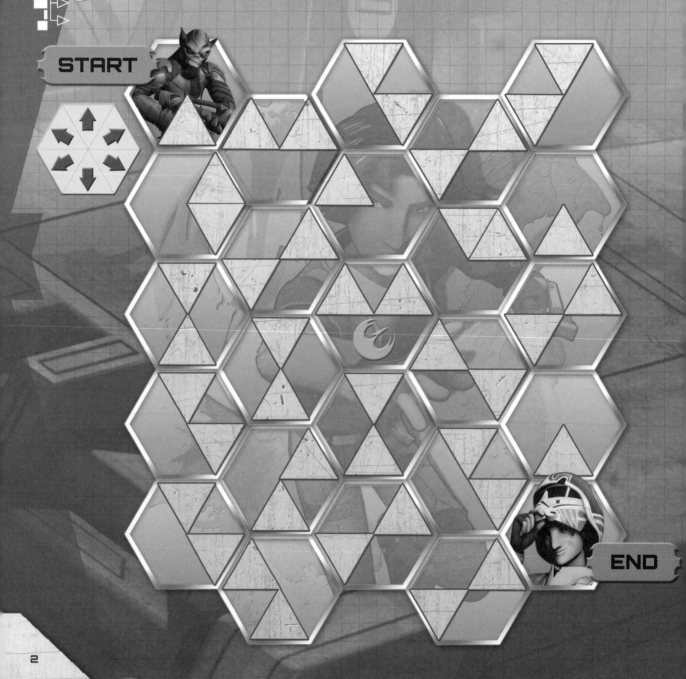

To keep Ezra from getting into trouble, Zeb locked him in a storage closet. That doesn't stop Ezra, who crawls through the maintenance ducts instead! Guide Ezra through the interior of the *Ghost* until you reach the END.

START

END

FIND THE IMPOSTERS!

Ezra has survived on his own for years, and is very good at disguises. Can you spot which one of these four Ezras is actually an imposter?

Kanan doesn't like to talk about his Jedi history. Even his old Jedi friends would hardly recognize him these days. Can you identify which image of Kanan is the imposter?

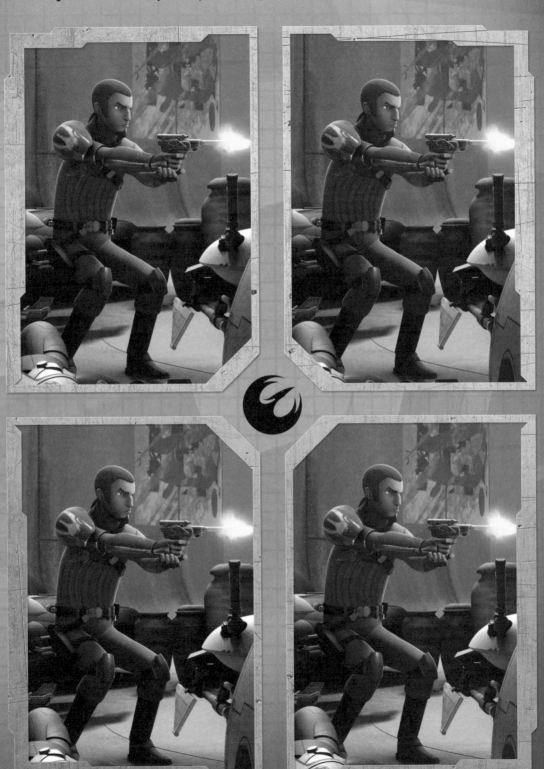

JEDI TRAINING
WORD SEARCH & SCRAMBLE

The rebels are blending into the crowd to escape from the Inquisitor. Using the picture key, can you find each sequence of Ezra, Kanan, Sabine, Zeb, Chopper, or Hera in the large image below? Look up, down, across, and diagonally.

PICTURE KEY

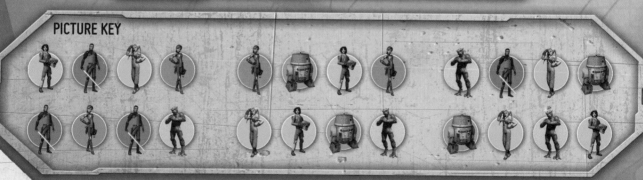

REBEL TRAINING LEVEL 1: Prove your skills as a rebel recruit by finding the words below that describe their struggle in the puzzle. Look up, down, across —— and even backward——to find the hidden words.

```
E Q R E B E L S F P F H D
V T U I B H Y M R T V I L S B
M E K Y S D E B I U H Q O X C
M N G I H B Q I I O U A T H P
I A R T U F B T X E X Z H N S
G D P R J P E Z R A S D A Q X
K R N O T A C O A K A D L I K
U D R O I D D T W W B O A U N
O M U P R C D O H G I T E C R
L S K E L V Y L L F N C T H P
W X G R T T U I U N E H I O A
C A C G H I A P M Z L E J D W
Z I H E K B U Q H Y A A S P V
U F C D F H E R A F D M L E K
L W P W B Z T B I B F S R
```

HERA	EZRA	SABINE
REBELS	CHOPPER	DROID
TROOPER	PILOT	LOTHAL

The Lothal marketplace is full of activity as merchants sell their goods under the eye of the Imperial supply master and his stormtrooper guards. From your vantage point on a nearby rooftop, spot these items before the Empire spots you! Look out! One of the items is not in the picture—can you identify which one?

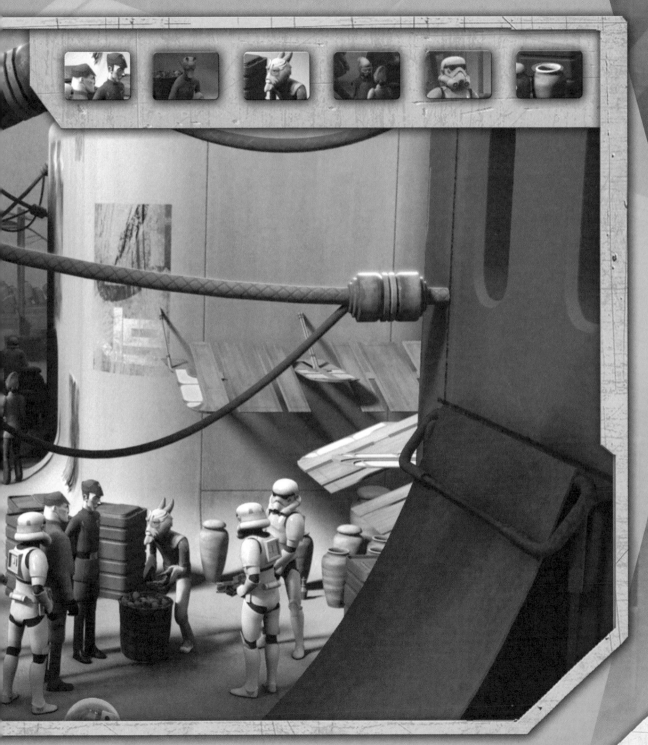

SHAPE SEARCH

The rebels have slipped into the shadows to escape from an Imperial patrol. Do you have the skills to identify Ezra, Kanan, Sabine, Zeb, and Hera only by their silhouettes?

The ability to quickly identify starships is important for any rebel. Can you match the images of the *Ghost*, the *Phantom*, the Imperial Star Destroyer, and the TIE fighter to the silhouettes below?

STAR WARS GRIDS

Below are six squares that are part of the big picture of Sabine's one-of-a-kind Mandalorian helmet. Can you identify where each square appears in the picture of Sabine on the right?

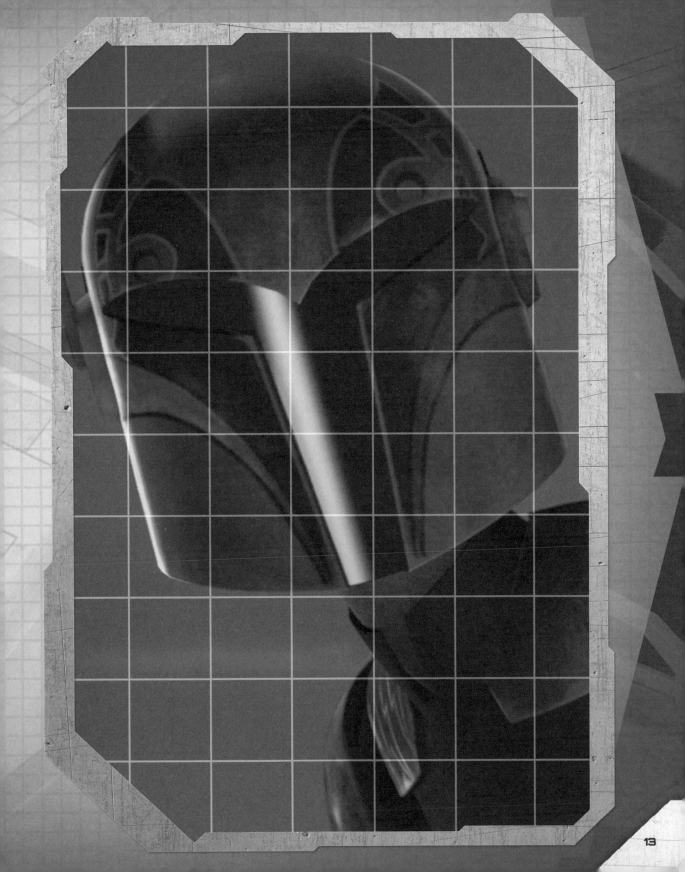

Chopper is a feisty little astromech droid who helps keep the *Ghost* in top shape. He's been patched together from lots of different parts over the years. Can you spot the five differences between the real Chopper on the left and the similar-looking droid on the right?

The Inquisitor tracks down and eliminates all threats to the Empire. He uses the dark side of the Force to trick and confuse his enemies. See past his illusions to find what five things are different about these two images of the Inquisitor.

LOTHAL MAZES

Ezra and Kanan are on a secret mission in the market district. They are far apart from each other and need to get crates full of supplies past Imperial stormtroopers. Find the paths that will take both rebels from their START positions to the safety of the *Ghost* in the center of the maze.

START

START

The *Ghost*'s deflector shields are acting up again. Can you help Chopper repair the *Ghost*'s circuit board before it's too late? Repair the circuit by finding the path from START to END.

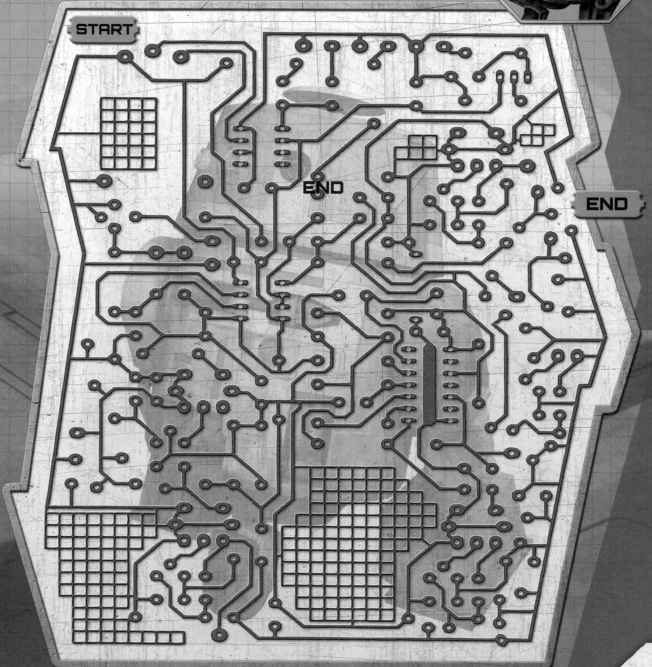

START

END

END

JEDI TRAINING
WORD SEARCH & SCRAMBLE

The Imperials need to be stopped before they leave Lothal with their Wookiee prisoners. Using the picture key, can you find each sequence of the Inquisitor, Agent Kallus, Grint, Aresko, or a stormtrooper in the large image below? Look up, down, across, and diagonally.

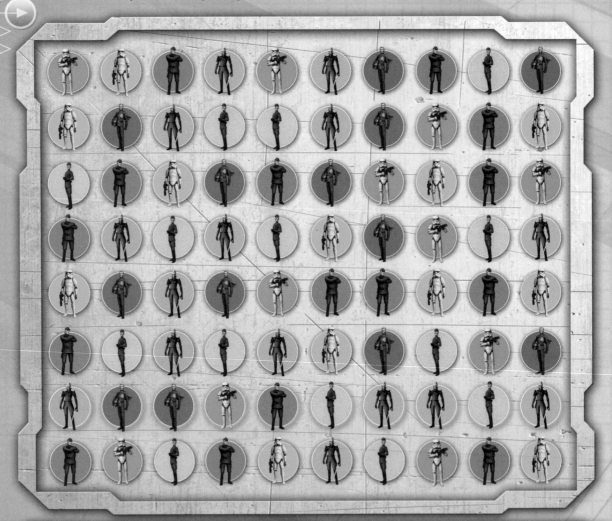

PICTURE KEY

REBEL TRAINING LEVEL 2: You're ready to learn the ways of the Jedi as you study with Kanan. In the puzzle, locate all the words below that relate to your Force training. Look up, down, across —and even backward—to find the words.

```
E C R O F L A K T D S F C M D
J L N Y H T I S E U S Y T G L
O D U Y Z T J L K A N A N J I
O C V P N P S F V D R Y E D G
M C H F Y H Y G V O Z B U D H
W T D Q D O Z R Q Y G H D K T
Z I G T A E Y D R A L O X V S
R X X L B T F E J I S L J Z A
I E L P M E T F G M Q O F V B
W Z S V B X Z S Y L Q C T D E
O Q L O P K T U T C M R D B R
V I A H I Y N D U M Z O W K Z
O S I G H B N T S C J N C W D
W Y R Q Z A L I I T G V X B I
W Y T S V N J E D I A F S B T
```

KANAN	JEDI	TEMPLE
LIGHTSABER	YODA	SITH
FORCE	HOLOCRON	TRIALS

21

Sabine and Chopper need to scan their surroundings to stay one step ahead of the Empire. Can you identify where the six squares below are located in the big picture at right?

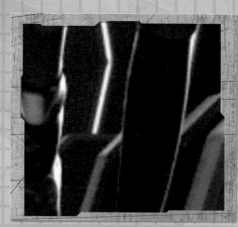

Ezra has always loved collecting stormtrooper helmets, and sometimes they come in handy as disguises. He hopes he can get past the Imperials without anyone discovering his true identity. Can you spot the six differences between these two images of Ezra?

Agent Kallus has received an important hologram message from the Inquisitor. Imperial crew members think the message might be a fake. Can you spot the six differences between these images before the Empire does?

LOTHAL MAZES

Kanan is teaching Ezra how to become a Jedi. By using the Force, Ezra hopes to unlock the secrets inside this Holocron. Help Ezra by finding the path through the maze that takes him from START to END. May the Force be with you!

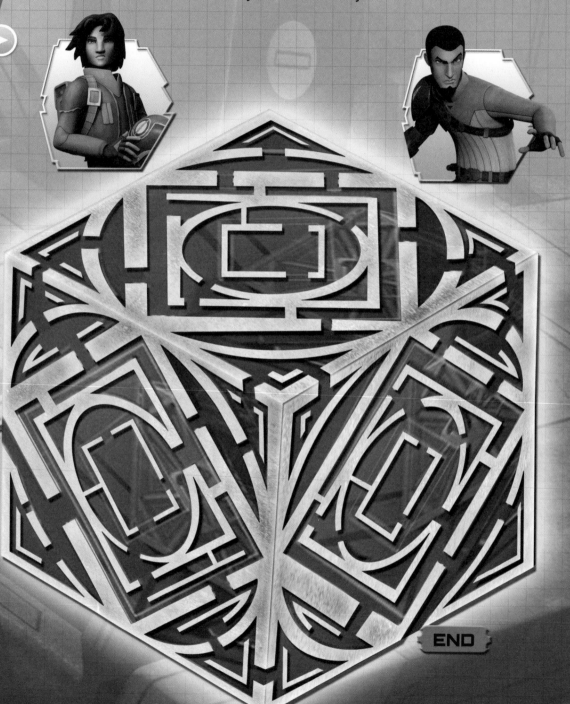

START

END

Your mission: Find your way through the maze and avoid the Empire's agents. You must follow a path from START to END, but you can only travel using the rebel symbols. You can move up, down, across, or diagonally. Good luck!

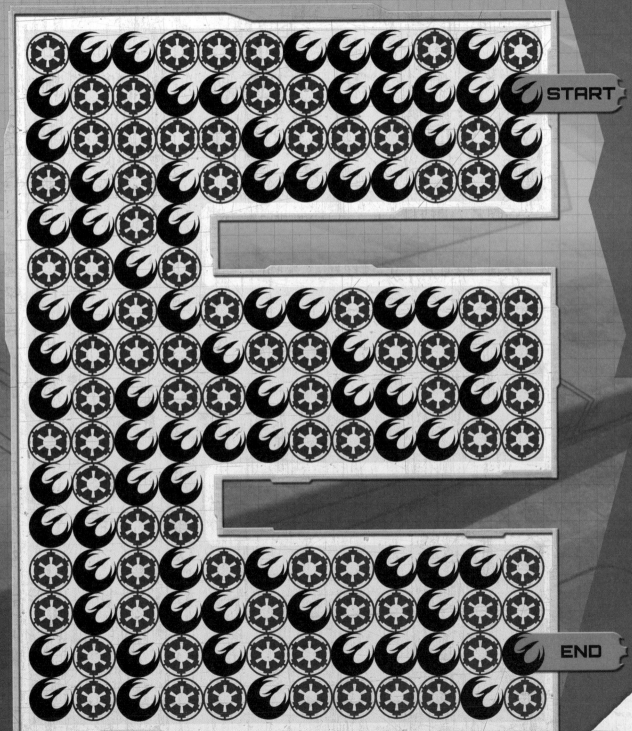

START

END

Many ships land on and take off from the spaceport in Lothal's Capital City. Using the picture key, can you find each sequence of starships in the large image below? Look up, down, across, and diagonally.

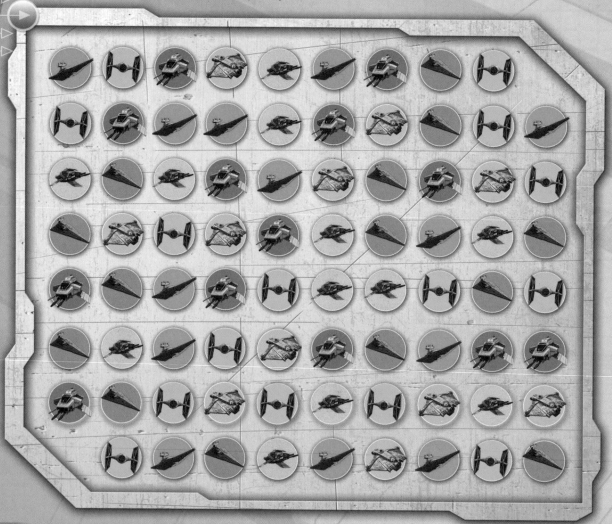

PICTURE KEY

REBEL TRAINING LEVEL 3: The galaxy is full of many different alien species who all live together. It is important to be able to identify these aliens if you see them. In this puzzle, find all the hidden words below. Remember to search up, down, across—and even backward.

```
N O X K N V J S Z Y K Q U W
C U T H O D T K E L I W T H Y
L T A T V E Z Z N R B Y G B
N O S O J V G O H R E C N I H
A F A I Q A T B Y R N R L I U
I Q L K I R E C J C J L R Y T
R V Y M C O P R F D A K L Q T
O D N O V N A A G J W Q R A T
L B D C N I V W I U N L E E Q
A N F A N A R A B M U Z E D M
D J Y N P N F J X M W P I P R
N Q R E M S N R G F Z P K P D
A P P C K T O J U S C K O Z W
M U O J J F A B N A I D O R K
T Y T Y X I I M L Y C W J
```

LASAT   MANDALORIAN   UMBARAN

RODIAN   WOOKIEE   DEVARONIAN

TWILEK   JAWA   HUTT

31

REBEL FIND-ITS

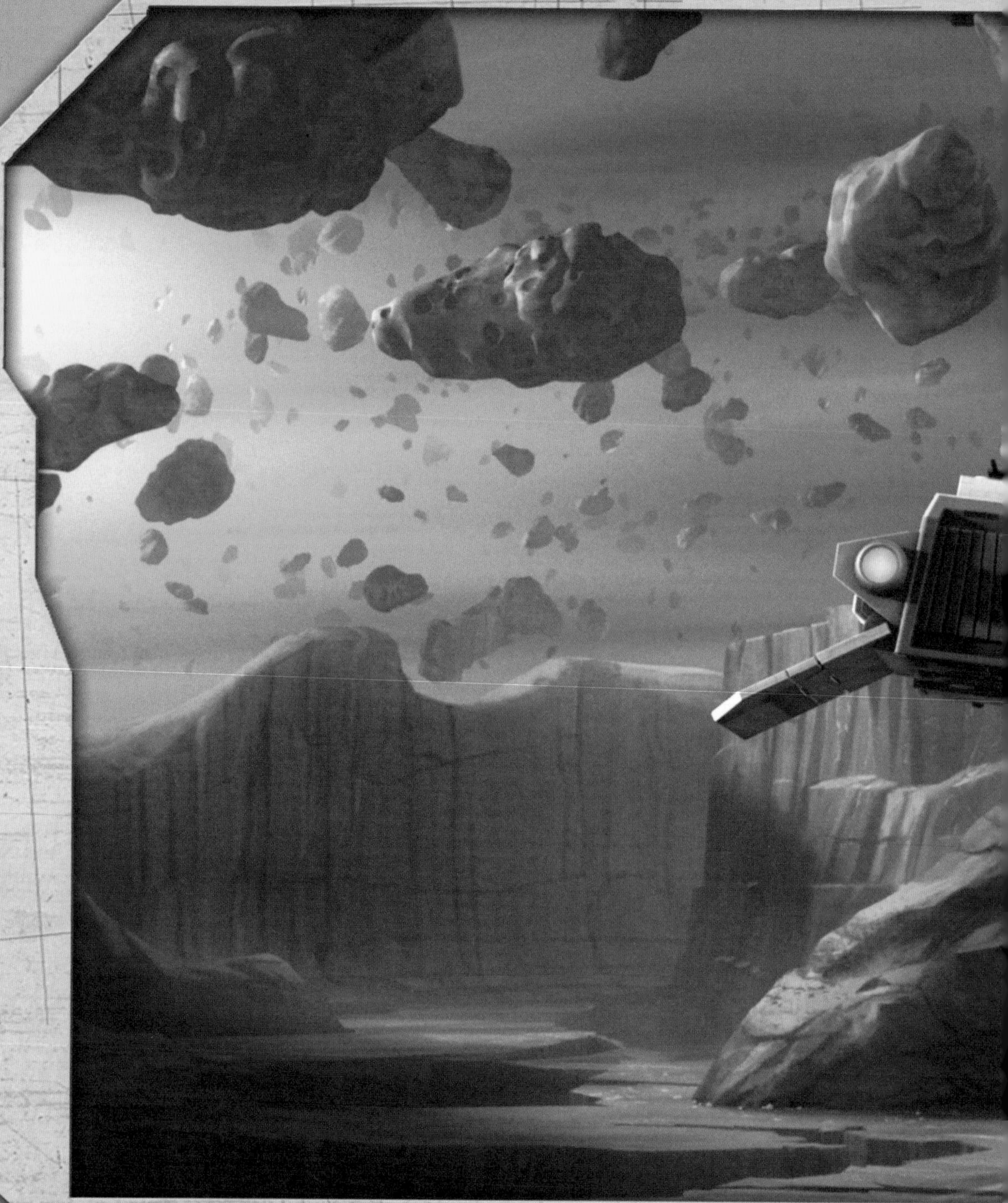

The *Phantom* is coming in for a landing at a secret base in an asteroid field. If one of the asteroids in the sky hits the ship, it's game over! Prove your skills as a rebel lookout by finding the following items in the scene below. Look out! One of the items is not in the picture—can you identify which one?

STAR WARS GRIDS

The Empire is on high alert! Stormtroopers are searching everywhere to find the rebels on Lothal. Can you find where the six squares below fit into the big picture on the right?

A group of stormtroopers is investigating some strange activity around their TIE fighters. By finding the seven differences between two scenes, they hope to find evidence of rebel sabotage. Can you spot the seven differences first?

Ezra found a helmet belonging to an Imperial TIE fighter pilot. When he puts it on, he sees strange computer readouts of his surroundings. Help Ezra make sense of what he's seeing by spotting the seven differences between these two images.

JEDI TRAINING
WORD SEARCH & SCRAMBLE

The rebels need all the friends they can get. Help them locate their allies by unscrambling the following names and writing the correct names in the spaces next to the scrambled versions.

ZARE   _ _ _ _

BETESO   _ _ _ _ _ _

ANAKN   _ _ _ _ _

NEISAB   _ _ _ _ _ _

EHPCPRO   _ _ _ _ _ _ _

EHRA   _ _ _ _

RCFULMU   _ _ _ _ _ _ _

BZE   _ _ _

REBEL TRAINING LEVEL 4: You've passed the previous challenges, and the rebels have given you top-secret information on Imperial activities. Find the words at the bottom of the page in the puzzle below. Unlike the earlier challenges, words can now appear diagonally!

```
B N N H O A Z F D O V X T V
V M I N Y C K D T E I H Z I H
S U K C A P W S K P T T N Z E
G O N D B K D W E S J E B P S
A H E K E L D E X R W K T M U
M M S I J N N R S K A A M N G
Y E Z Y E W P H Y T S M Y T N
N F A D I Z J V N B R R N I K
L M K F Z K H Z Q P B O K K O
I N Q U I S I T O R L R Y K E
N H S U L L A K M M A B I E R
H T C Z Q H B N E T S M L R R
U G R I N T I S M O T S X H O
B G M J J G Z R M W E F Z T X
C T M T R U F J M Q R Y L U
```

INQUISITOR
KALLUS
GRINT

DESTROYER
ARESKO
MAKETH

TARKIN
BLASTER
ACADEMY

STAR WARS GRIDS

The Inquisitor is one of the Empire's most dangerous agents. Rebels need to learn to recognize his face if they don't want to be captured. See if you can identify where the six squares below are located in the large picture of the Inquisitor on the right.

LOTHAL MAZES

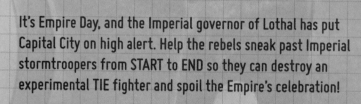

It's Empire Day, and the Imperial governor of Lothal has put Capital City on high alert. Help the rebels sneak past Imperial stormtroopers from START to END so they can destroy an experimental TIE fighter and spoil the Empire's celebration!

START

END

The Inquisitor has come to Lothal to hunt the rebels. Follow the pattern on the right to help the rebels reach safety. You can go down, left, and right—but not diagonally. Whatever you do, avoid the Inquisitor!

START

END

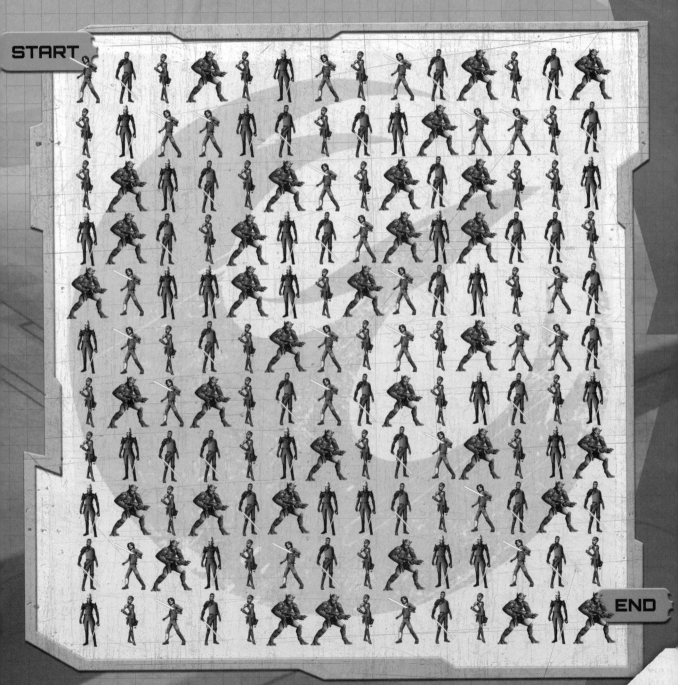

FIND THE IMPOSTERS!

It can be hard to tell one Imperial from another, especially when they're wearing armor. Can you figure out which of these images of Agent Kallus is actually an imposter?

The Empire wants to arrest Zeb for stealing valuable cargo. They found these four images of Zeb, but one is actually an imposter. Can you find it?

JEDI TRAINING
WORD SEARCH & SCRAMBLE

The Empire is scrambling its transmissions, hoping to keep its secrets safe from the rebels. Crack the Empire's code by unscrambling the words below and writing the correct word next to the scrambled version.

LUAKLS — _ _ _ _ _ _

OTREOPR — _ _ _ _ _ _ _

POLIT — _ _ _ _ _

INGRT — _ _ _ _ _

AROKSE — _ _ _ _ _ _

YTELS — _ _ _ _ _

KEHTAM — _ _ _ _ _ _

COFEFRI — _ _ _ _ _ _ _

REBEL TRAINING LEVEL 5: The rebels don't spend all their time on Lothal. In the puzzle below, locate all the words related to space travel at the bottom of the page. Remember to search up, down, across, diagonally, and even backward.

```
F O A L M H I D B N T K O B L
M R Z G O Y M J I Z A J E L O
O K W U V P Y T X O G O I K O
T P O G D E S C J O R G J I H
N D S H U R D P J R H E A O B
A B R O R D Y G A T V R T J Z
H L X S V R G W S X G Z T S J
P T B T C I V P G A L A X Y A
C L C M W V E G N I K A O L C
Y O A J N E T J P U B M E F A
E W G N D X Y M X M R S N X M
E L I X E Z Z G Y W S R F W R
S G U A O T Y Z T E P V A E D
Z M C K B R S M K H V W J Y G
M Z F W M V I Q B S D C F
```

HYPERDRIVE	GALAXY	PHANTOM
GHOST	LIGHTSPEED	ASTEROID
KESSEL	CLOAKING	PLANET

The people of Lothal are easily distracted—and so are the city's Imperial rulers. While the rebels create a diversion, find the following items in the image below. Be sure to finish before the stormtroopers notice something is wrong! Look out! One of the items is not in the picture—can you identify which one?

STAR WARS GRIDS

When Zeb rushes into a fight, it's always bad news for the Empire! See if you can locate the six squares below in the big picture of Zeb on the right, before things get too crazy in the big brawl that's sure to happen next.

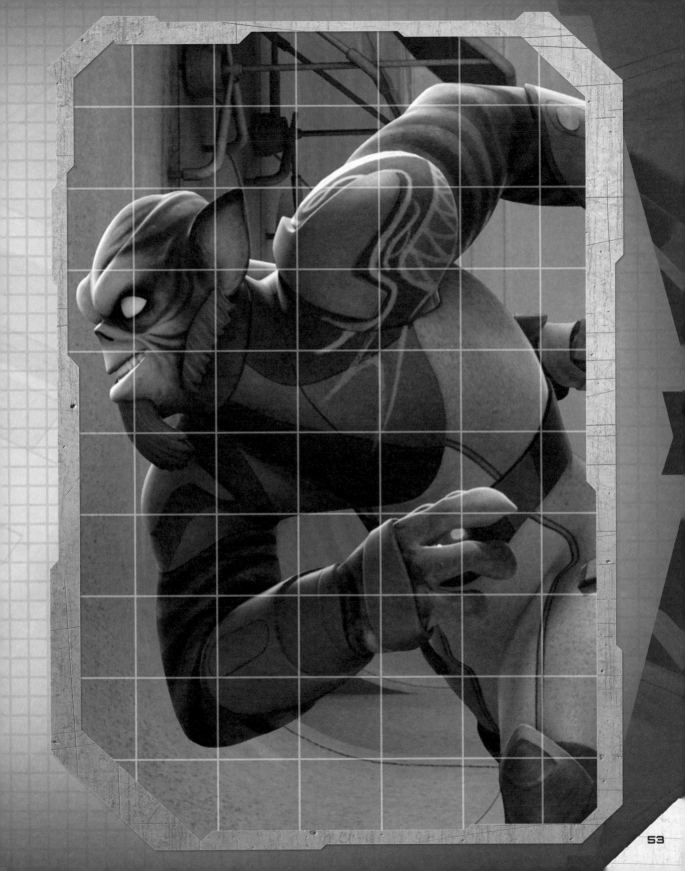

The gravity aboard the Imperial freighter has gone out, leaving Agent Kallus and his stormtroopers floating in midair! Agent Kallus is disoriented and trying to figure out what happened. Can you spot the eight differences between these two images?

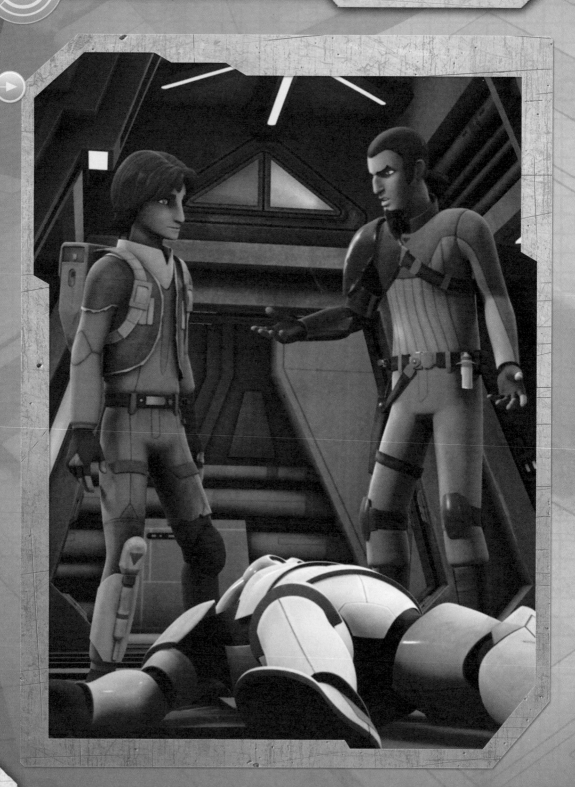

Kanan and Ezra have knocked out one stormtrooper—but more are on the way. They need to figure out what to do, and fast. Can you help them by spotting the eight differences between these two images?

LOTHAL MAZES

Ezra has gone undercover inside the Imperial Academy. In this training exercise, he needs to reach the top of the wall by following the pattern of helmets at the right. Start at the green arrow and end at the red arrow. Don't stop until the end!

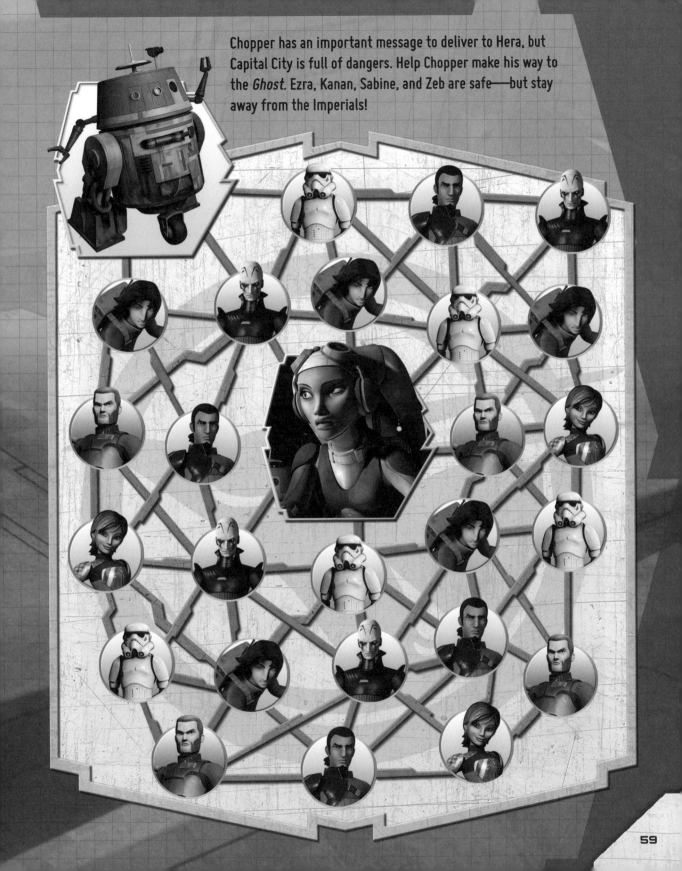

Chopper has an important message to deliver to Hera, but Capital City is full of dangers. Help Chopper make his way to the *Ghost*. Ezra, Kanan, Sabine, and Zeb are safe—but stay away from the Imperials!

FIND THE IMPOSTERS!

The rebels need to pull Ezra aboard the *Ghost* so they can escape. But first they must be sure they're rescuing the right Ezra! Can you help them discover which of these Ezras is the imposter?

Ezra is training to become a Jedi. He must have sharp eyes and a clear mind to avoid the illusions of the dark side. Can you see which of these Ezras is actually an imposter?

JEDI TRAINING
WORD SEARCH & SCRAMBLE

The rebels are planning a big operation for Empire Day. The details have been scrambled to keep the Empire from learning their plans. Unscramble the words below and write the correct words next to them.

OLHLTA — _ _ _ _ _ _

LAAPTCI — _ _ _ _ _ _ _

AMTERK — _ _ _ _ _ _

AGTSBAEO — _ _ _ _ _ _ _ _

AGURD — _ _ _ _ _

NIPOESLXO — _ _ _ _ _ _ _ _ _

SPAEEC — _ _ _ _ _ _

OTPLAR — _ _ _ _ _ _

REBEL TRAINING LEVEL 6: In your final challenge, you must learn that the rebels are fighting for the entire galaxy—not just Lothal. In the puzzle below, find the important words related to the rebel struggle at the bottom of the page. Remember to search up, down, across, diagonally, and even backward.

```
F R A U I C K L O L N Q K L R
S I E I B E M E P J O M Q Y I
B C K D N M Z H W F I R O J D
C E D O A H K A P H L P K S Z
K K B P A V Q A F D L E M X P
N I D H H D R O D E E M C S A
K A N X F V I K N E B P U N A
F J I V E L A I T Q E E T X B
X Q M S Z P T L U T R R Z D P
H W K G S A Y E D U Q O U F I
F U F M P I K G R E X R D E X
O L X L D X R P E L R Q I H J
L L A M H D K L W A N A G R O
N P C O R U S C A N T U A P A
J R G N M Q J F Q C Q D Z N N
```

KENOBI   VADER   ORGANA

REBELLION   EMPEROR   CALRISSIAN

PALPATINE   CORUSCANT   ALDERAAN

63

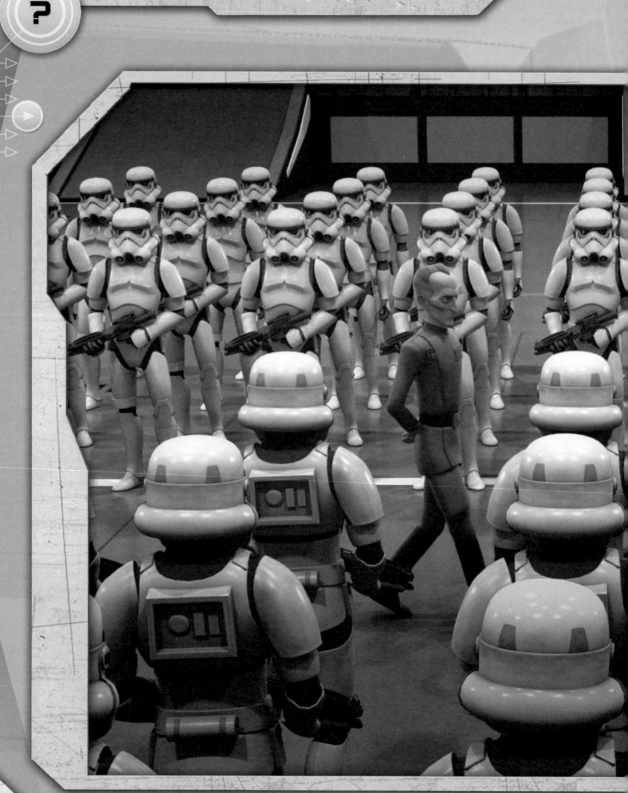

If you want to become a rebel, it is important to identify Imperials by sight. Many high-ranking Imperials are present at this meeting. Can you identify a TIE pilot, a transport driver, Agent Kallus, the Inquisitor, Tarkin, and Maketh Tua?

TIE pilot   Transport driver   Agent Kallus   The Inquisitor   Tarkin   Maketh Tua

SHAPE SEARCH

Sabine has intercepted an Imperial transmission, but the images have been scrambled. Using the pictures below, can you match each Imperial character to the correct swirled image?

The rebels are taking cover as they prepare for their next mission. Only their shadows are visible. Using the pictures below of a Wookiee, Sabine, Zeb, Ezra, and Chopper, can you match each character to the correct shadow?

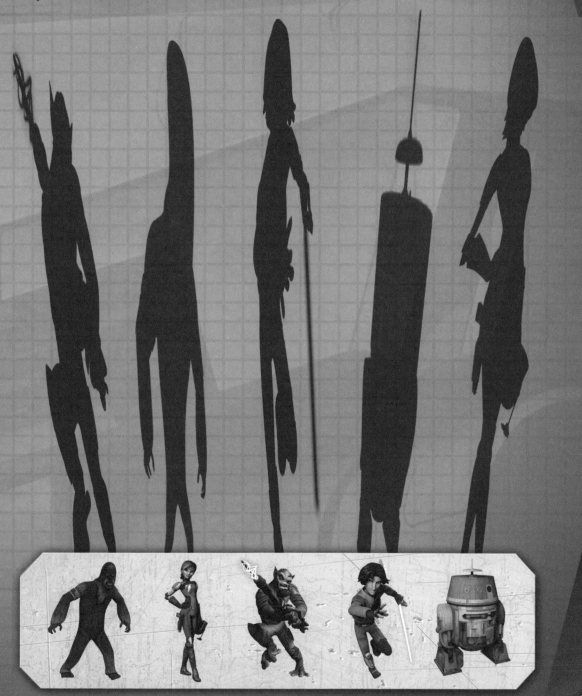

STAR WARS GRIDS

Kanan doesn't like to reveal his Jedi background——but if he wants to help his friends he has no choice. The stormtroopers are amazed at the sight of a Jedi lightsaber. Before they attack, try to locate the six squares below in the big picture on the right.

The lightsaber is the weapon of a Jedi, but it can be tough to tell whether a lightsaber is a genuine Jedi artifact or a cheap copy. Help Ezra by spotting the nine differences between the two images.

Sabine is ready for action, but waits to get her orders from Hera first. The Empire is using a jammer and Hera's transmission is hard to hear. Help Sabine decrypt the message by spotting the nine differences between the two images.

JEDI MIND TRICKS
TRIVIA Q&A

Take this *Rebels* trivia test! See how many questions you can answer correctly.
Answers are on page 96.

1. Ezra's home planet is called _____.
   a. Alderaan
   b. Ryloth
   c. Lothal

2. The Empire's primary starfighter is the _____.
   a. T–16 Skyhopper
   b. TIE fighter
   c. X-wing fighter

3. Chopper is _____ droid.
   a. an astromech
   b. a protocol
   c. a battle

4. Hera is a member of the _____ species.
   a. Gungan
   b. Twi'lek
   c. Neimoidian

5. The rebels fly around in a starship named the _____.
   a. *Falcon*
   b. *Ghost*
   c. *Shark*

6. _____ can use the dark side of the Force.
   a. Sabine
   b. The Inquisitor
   c. Tseebo

7. Agent Kallus works for the _____.
   a. Republic Senate
   b. Imperial Security Bureau
   c. Mining Guild

8. _____ is the rebels' main pilot.
   a. Yoda
   b. Hera
   c. Zeb

9. Imperial AT-DP walkers have _____ legs.
   a. two
   b. four
   c. eight

10. _____ likes to collect stormtrooper helmets.
    a. Aresko
    b. Chopper
    c. Ezra

11. Ezra's rebel call sign is _____ .
   a. Specter 6
   b. Star 6
   c. Speeder 6

12. _____ is one of the two droids who accidentally joins up with the rebels on Garel.
   a. EV-9D9
   b. C-3PO
   c. R4-P17

13. Zeb's special weapon is called a _____ .
   a. bo-rifle
   b. bowcaster
   c. lightsaber

14. Hera and Sabine are attacked by _____ at an asteroid base.
   a. rancors
   b. tauntauns
   c. fyrnocks

15. _____ uses a double-bladed lightsaber with a spinning handle.
   a. Hondo Ohnaka
   b. The Inquisitor
   c. Darth Vader

16. A _____ is a device that stores and plays back Jedi secrets.
   a. holocron
   b. comlink
   c. blaster

17. _____ loves to tag Imperial buildings with graffiti.
   a. Lyste
   b. Kanan
   c. Sabine

18. Zeb is an alien known as _____.
   a. a Lasat
   b. a Quarren
   c. a Jawa

19. _____ is the rebel who specializes in explosives.
   a. Yoda
   b. Kanan
   c. Sabine

20. _____ once trained to become a Jedi.
   a. Zeb
   b. Kanan
   c. Agent Kallus

21. _____ goes undercover as a cadet at the Lothal Imperial Academy.
   a. Zeb
   b. Ezra
   c. Depa Billaba

22. The rebels try to rescue a Jedi Master from a prison called _____.
   a. the Spire
   b. the Wheel
   c. the Tire

23. Sabine wears _____ armor.
   a. Imperial
   b. Naboo
   c. Mandalorian

24. Ezra's birthday is on _____, which celebrates the founding of the Empire.
   a. Empire Day
   b. Coruscant Day
   c. Kallus Day

25. The rebels rescue a group of_____ from the spice mines of Kessel.
   a. Ewoks
   b. Wampas
   c. Wookiees

26. The *Ghost* has a detachable starfighter called the _____.
   a. *Phantom*
   b. *Nashtah*
   c. *Mynock*

27. _____ sometimes uses an energy slingshot.
   a. Ezra
   b. Hera
   c. Governor Pryce

28. _____ is the Devaronian crime boss of Lothal.
   a. Jabba
   b. Vizago
   c. Ziro

29. Kanan's lightsaber has a_____ –colored blade.
   a. red
   b. yellow
   c. blue

30. _____ is the code name of Hera's secret contact.
   a. Fulcrum
   b. Fluffy
   c. Fett

31. Ezra sees a Jedi named _____ in a recorded message.
   a. Yaddle
   b. Obi-Wan Kenobi
   c. Saesee Tiin

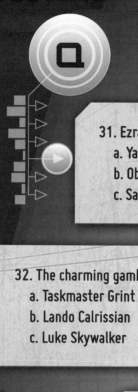

32. The charming gambler _____ convinces the rebels to sneak a cargo past the Empire.
   a. Taskmaster Grint
   b. Lando Calrissian
   c. Luke Skywalker

33. _____ is famous for broadcasting anti-Empire messages .
   a. Bib Fortuna
   b. Boss Nass
   c. Gall Trayvis

34. Commandant _____ is in charge of Lothal's Imperial Academy.
   a. Poggle
   b. Lobot
   c. Aresko

35. _____ are huge, triangular Imperial battleships.
   a. Star Destroyers
   b. Death Stars
   c. Blockade Runners

USE THE FORCE
MEMORY CHALLENGE

TEST YOUR FORCE POWERS WITH THIS JEDI MEMORY CHALLENGE
Lift the flaps two at a time and see what's underneath. If you find a matching pair, leave the
flaps up. If they're not a match, close the flaps. Then keep lifting the flaps two at a time to
find all the matching pairs of symbols.

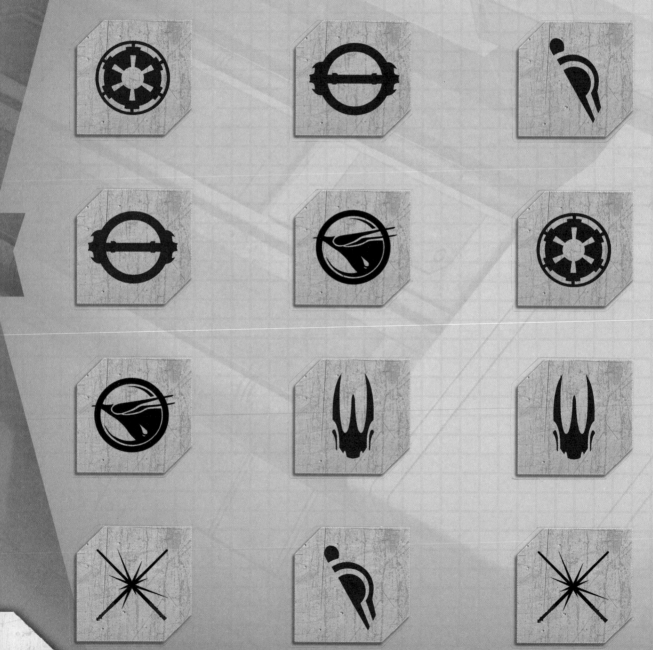

MEMORY CHALLENGE 2: JEDI PADAWAN

You've proven your Force sensitivity with the first memory challenge. Now see how long it takes you to find all the matching symbols in this challenge.

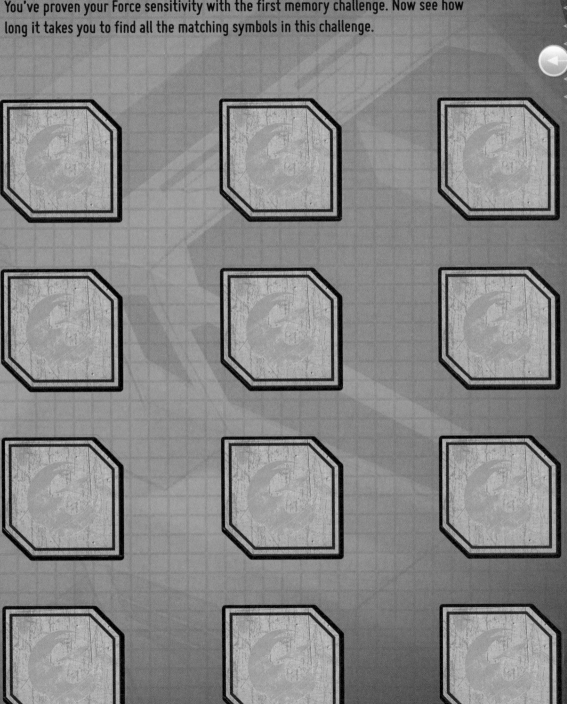

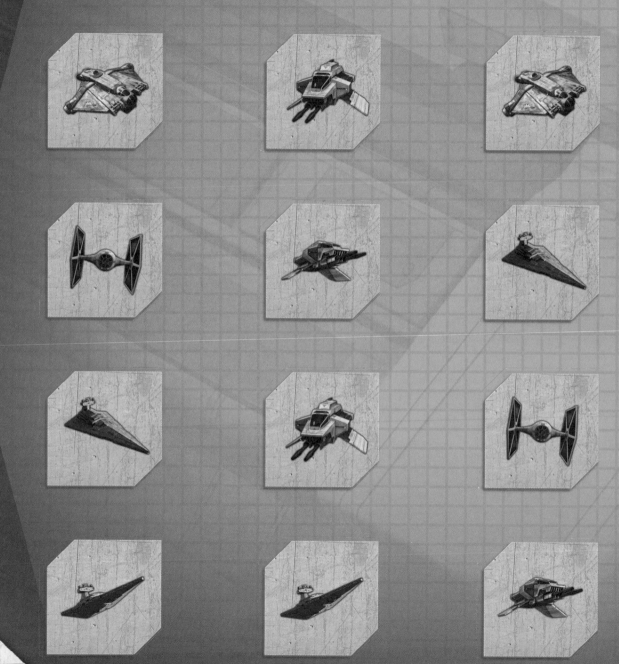

MEMORY CHALLENGE 3: JEDI KNIGHT

Now that you've passed the first two memory challenges, you're ready to take the Jedi trials. Find all the matching pairs of symbols in this challenge and earn the rank of Jedi Knight.

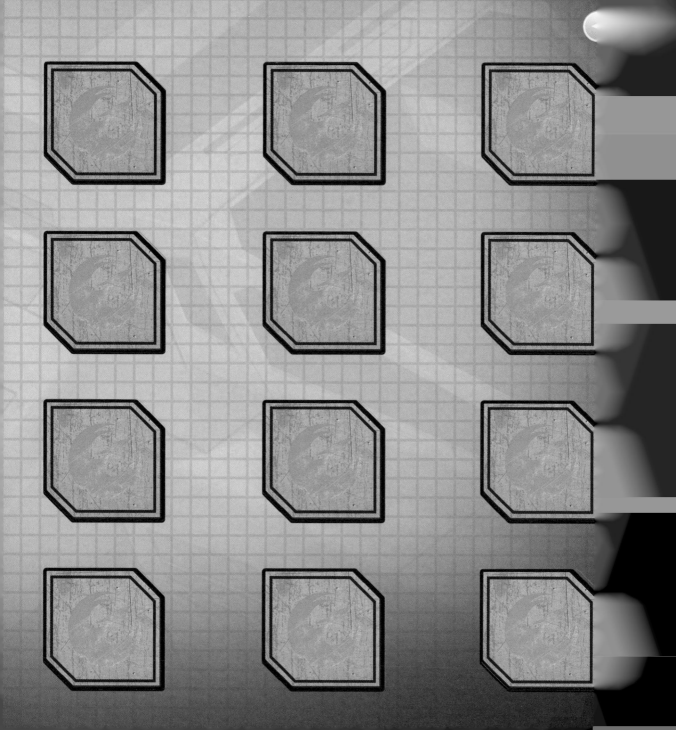

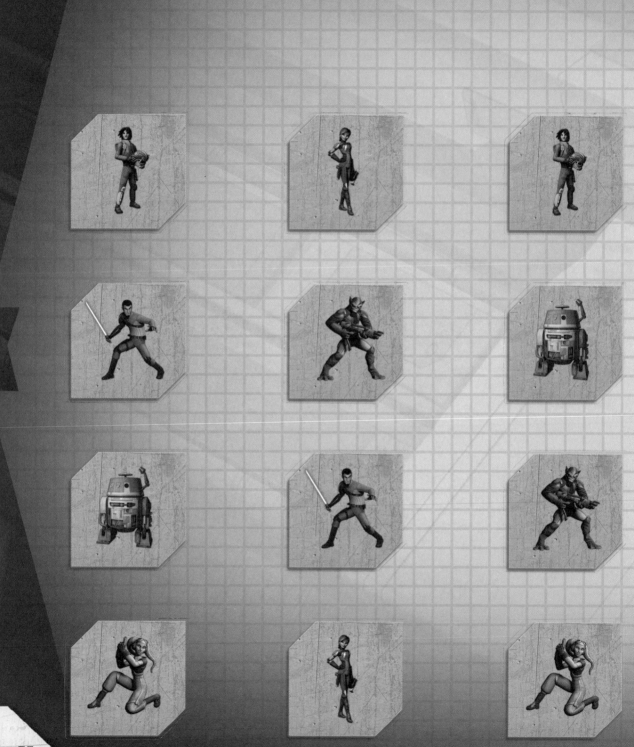

MEMORY CHALLENGE 4: JEDI MASTER

Are you ready for the final trial? Now that you've completed the previous challenges, see how fast you can find the matching pairs of symbols in this ultimate challenge. May the Force be with you!

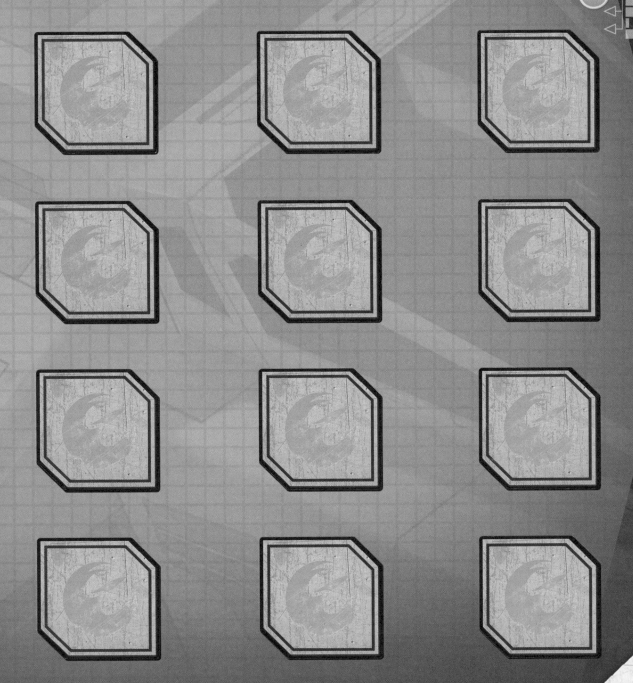

ANSWERS

⟳ 2

⟳ 3

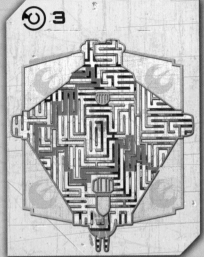

♣ 4

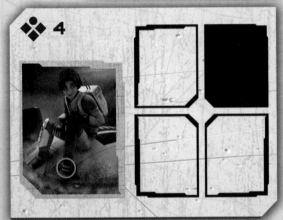

♣ 5

6

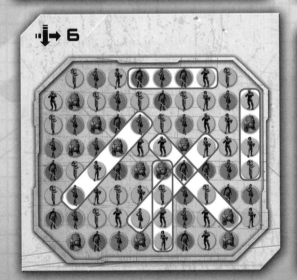

7

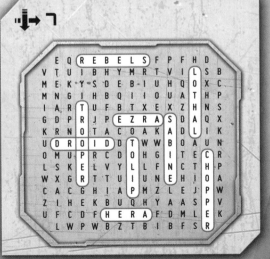

Word search words: REBELS, LOTHAL, TROOPER, EZRA, SABINE, DROID, TOLIP, CHOPPER, HERA

10

11

12-13

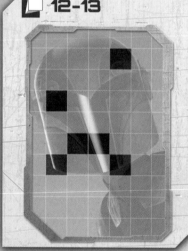

14-15

16-17

18

19

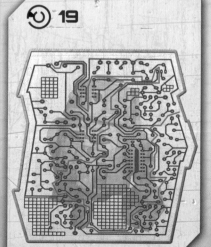

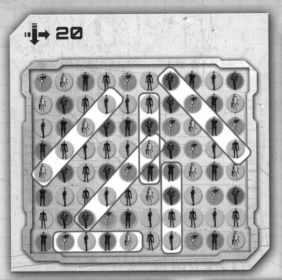

⇥ 20

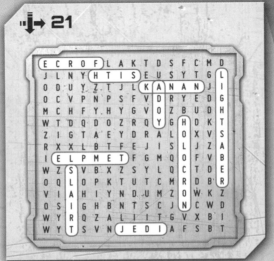

⇥ 21

```
E C R O F L A K T D S F C M D
J L N Y H T I S E U S Y T G L
O D U Y Z T J L K A N A N J I
O C V P N P S F V D O Y R Y E G
M C H F H Y H Y G V Z B U D H
W T D Q D O Z R Q Y G H O D K T
Z I G T A E Y D R A L H O X J S
R X X L B T F E J I S V Z A
I E L P M E T F G M Q O F V B
W Z S V B X Z S Y L Q C T D E
O L O P K T U T C M U Z M O W R
V I S H I Y N D U M Z W K Z
O B I G H B N T S C J N C W D
W Y R Q Z A L I I T G V X B I
W Y T S V N J E D I A F S B T
```

22-23

24-25

26-27

28

29

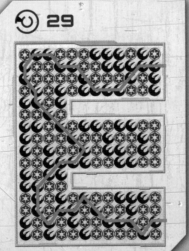

30

 31

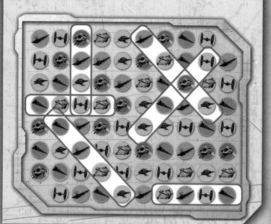

```
N O X K N V J S Z Y K Q U W
C L   T H O D   T K E L I W T   H Y
U T O T A S A L   D E V A R O N   G B
T O F Q I Q I   G O H R E C N I   U Y
L Q V K I C   T B Y R N R L   H U T T
N A F M O C   E C J C J L R   Q T Q
A D I N D C V N I   A Q J W Q   E M R
I Y N A F A   A W I U N L E   A D P
R J Y N W   N A R A B M U   Z E I K   M R D
O M Q S Z   N F J X M W P   R A W
L P K O   S N R G F Z P   O W K
A U O Z W   T D J U S C K
D J J F A B   N A I D O W   R K
N Q T Y X I I M L Y C W J
```

? 32-33

◻ 34-35

🔍 36-37

🔍 38-39

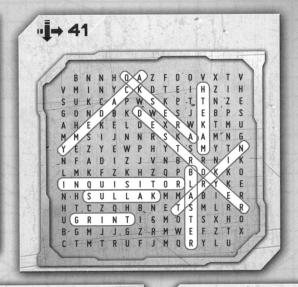

40

EZRA
TSEEBO
KANAN
SABINE
CHOPPER
HERA
FULCRUM
ZEB

41

```
B N N H Q A Z F D O V X T V
V M I N Y C K D T E I H Z H
S U K C A P W S K P T N Z E
G O N D B K D W E S E K B P S
A H E K E L D E X R W A K T M
M M S I J N N R S K A M T N G
Y E Z Y E W P H Y T S A E M N
N F A D I Z V N B R R N I K
L M K F Z K H Z Q P B O K R Y
I N Q U I S I T O R L R Y K E
N H S U L L A K M M A B I E
H T C Z Q H B N E T S M L R
U G R I N T I S M O R S X H O
B G M J J G Z R M W E F Z T X
C T M T R U F J M Q R Y L U
```

42-43

44

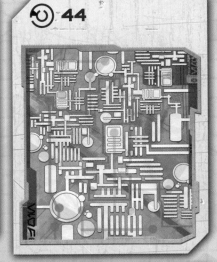

45

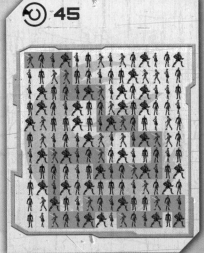

46

47

48

KALLUS
TROOPER
PILOT
GRINT
ARESKO
LYSTE
MAKETH
OFFICER

49

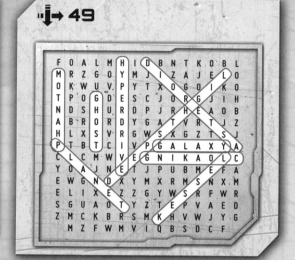

? 50-51

52-53

54-55

56-57

58

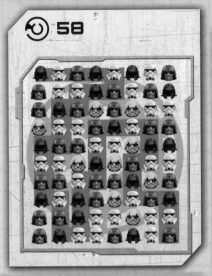

59

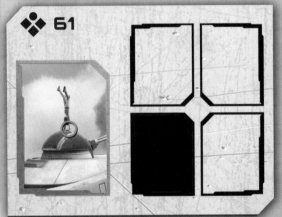

60

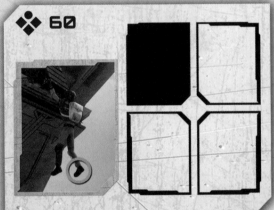

61

62

LOTHAL

CAPITAL

MARKET

SABOTAGE

GUARD

EXPLOSION

ESCAPE

PATROL

63

```
F R A U I C K L O L N Q K L R
S I E I B E M E P J O M Q Y I
B C K D N M Z H W F I R O J D
C E D O A H K A P H L P K S Z
K K B P A V Q A F D E M X X Z
N I D H D R D O D E E M E R
K A N X F V I K N E B P U N A
F J I V E L A I T Q E P T X B
X Q M S Z P T L U T R Z D Z
H W K G S A Y E D U Q O U F I
F U F M P I K G R E X O D E X
O L X L D X R P E L R Q I H J
L N L L A M H D K L W A N A G R O
N P C O R U S C A N T U A P A
J R G N M Q J Z C Z N N
```

? 64-65

66

67

68-69

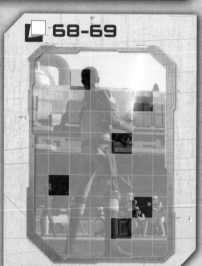

70-71

72-73

Q 74-80

1. c	8. b	15. b	22. a	29. c
2. b	9. a	16. a	23. c	30. a
3. a	10. c	17. c	24. a	31. b
4. b	11. a	18. a	25. c	32. b
5. b	12. b	19. c	26. a	33. c
6. b	13. a	20. b	27. a	34. c
7. b	14. c	21. b	28. b	35. a